Barry Bigfoot's Christmas Special

Written & Illustrated
by
Marcus Holly

Barry's night before Christmas

T'was the night before Christmas, and all through the land.
All creatures were peaceful; nothing was out of hand.
Most were resting in their dens,
without a care.
Except for Barry Bigfoot, he was enjoying the cold night air.

Barry walked quietly; he knew
most were snug in their beds.
He dared not interrupt the
sweet dreams that danced in
their heads.
When out of the night, arose
such a clatter.
Barry sprang into action to
see
what was the matter.

Away from his walk,
Barry flew like a flash.
Quickly, quietly,
dodging brush to avoid
a crash.
Barry paused at a tree
to see the moon lit
snow.
The reflection of the
light lit up the area
with a soft glow.

What to Barry's
wondering eyes should
appear, but a
marvelous sleigh and
eight magical reindeer.
With a robust driver, so
agile and quick.
Barry knew in an
instant, it must be St.
Nick.
Swifter than lighting,
his magical beasts
came.
Santa whistled and
called them by name.

Now Dasher, now Dancer,
now Prancer and Vixen.
On Comet, on Cupid, on
Donner and Blitzen.
To the top of the trees,
let's leave like the fall.
Now dash away, dash
away, dash away all.
Barry stood in
amazement as he
watched them fly.
No obstacle to slow them
as they breezed through
the sky.

Towards a tiny trotter
home, they flew.
With a sleigh filled
with gifts and St. Nick,
too.
Barry saw the odd
crew land on the tiny
trotter roof.
He admired the
reindeer formation
down to the hoof.

St. Nick grabbed his bag, then left his sleigh with a bound.
Past his team and down the smokestack without a sound.
Barry looked through the window and saw him clothed in fur, from head to foot.
With red clothing covered in ashes and soot.

He lowered the bundle that was on his back.
He favored a camper opening his overstuffed pack.
Barry saw how Santa's eyes twinkled, and his dimples looked merry.
His cheeks were rosy, and his nose like a holly berry.

His teeth in his grin resembled the moons light.
The hair on his face was just as white.
A fancy pipe he held in his teeth.
While smoke encircled his head like a wreath.
He had a strong, kind, face, and a large round belly.
It shook when he laughed, like a bowl full of jelly.
Barry thought he looked strong rather than plump.
Even though Barry smiled when he saw him, he knew Santa was no chump.
With a wink of his eye and twist of his head.
Barry was given assurance he had nothing to dread.

St. Nick didn't speak
and went straight to
work.
He placed presents
and filled stockings,
then turned with a
jerk.
He placed his finger on
the side of his nose.
He gave Barry a nod,
then up through the
fireplace he rose.

He hopped in his sleigh and tossed Barry a gift.
Gave his team a whistle and the sleigh started to lift.
Barry heard him call as they rose out of sight, "Merry Christmas to all and to all a good night".

Merry Christmas
and
Happy New
Year

www.ingramcontent.com/pod-product-compliance
Lightning Source LLC
LaVergne TN
LVHW021325160826
845679LV00001B/477

* 9 7 9 8 3 6 2 9 1 1 4 3 0 *